Do-It-Yourself Science™

EXPERIMENTS About PLANET EARTH

Zella Williams

PowerKiDS press.

New York

Published in 2007 by The Rosen Publishing Group, Inc.
29 East 21st Street, New York, NY 10010

First Edition

Editor: Joanne Randolph
Book Design: Greg Tucker and Ginny Chu
Photo Researcher: Sam Cha

Photo Credits: Cover © sgame/shutterstock.com; p. 5 © Royalty-Free/Photodisc; pp. 6–19 by Cindy Reiman; pp. 20–21 by Adriana Skura.

Library of Congress Cataloging-in-Publication Data

Williams, Zella.
  Experiments about planet Earth / Zella Williams. – 1st ed.
    p. cm. – (Do-it-yourself science)
  Includes index.
  ISBN-13: 978-1-4042-3662-2 (library binding)
  ISBN-10: 1-4042-3662-7 (library binding)
  1. Earth–Juvenile literature. 2. Astronomy–Experiments–Juvenile literature. 3. Earth sciences–Experiments–Juvenile literature. I. Title.
  QB631.4.W555 2007
  550.78–dc22
                                        2006026441

Manufactured in the United States of America

Contents

One Great Big Neighborhood

What do you have in common with everyone else in the world? We all live on the **planet** Earth. There is so much to learn about Earth, it is hard to know where to begin.

The first step is to look around. What do you see? What do you want to know about what you see? **Scientists** ask questions, too. They find the answers to their questions by doing **experiments**. Let's do some experiments that will help us learn about Earth.

Here we can see Earth (left) next to the Moon. The Moon moves around Earth, and Earth moves around the Sun.

Mapping Our Solar System

Everything in our **solar system** orbits, or moves around, the Sun. The Sun is a star that is very close to Earth. We get heat, light, and **energy** from the Sun. The planets that orbit the Sun include Mercury, Venus, Earth, Mars, Jupiter, Saturn, Uranus, and Neptune. Let's make a map of our solar system.

You will need

- a basketball
- a grapefruit
- an apple
- two plums
- two small marbles
- two peas

Note: The pictures on page 7 do not show the actual spacing of objects for space reasons.

1 Find some open space about 30 yards (27 m) long. Playgrounds and parks are good places. Walk to one end and put down the basketball. The basketball stands for the Sun. Each object you use stands for a planet. The size difference between the objects gives you an idea of the different size of the planets.

2

Starting at the basketball, take one step and put down a pea for Mercury. Take another step and put down a marble for Venus. Take a half step from Venus and put down the other marble for Earth, where we live. Each step you take stands for about 36 million miles (58 million km) in our solar system.

3

From Earth take one and a half steps and put down a pea for Mars. Now take nine steps and put down the grapefruit for Jupiter. Go 11 steps and set down the apple for Saturn.

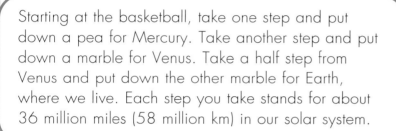

4

Walk 24 steps and put down a plum for Uranus. Take 27 more steps and put down the other plum for Neptune. For a long time, scientists also included Pluto on the list of planets. Pluto is now thought of as a dwarf planet. Step back and take a look. You have mapped the planets in our solar system!

The Parts of Earth

Earth has three main layers, or thicknesses. In the center of our planet is the **core**, or the first layer. The core is a ball of iron. The layer around the core is the **mantle**. The top layer of Earth is the **crust**, where we live. Follow these steps to learn more about Earth's layers.

You will need

- a hard-boiled egg
- a knife

1 Carefully break the shell of a hard-boiled egg but do not remove the shell. Have an adult help you cut the egg in half, along the long side.

2 Look at the yellow yolk of the egg. The size and shape stand for Earth's iron core. The core is about 2,000 miles (3,219 km) thick.

3 Look at the white part of the egg. It goes around the yolk in the same way that the mantle goes around Earth's core. However, Earth's mantle is molten, or made of melted rock. The mantle is 1,800 miles (2,897 km) thick.

4 The egg shell is like Earth's crust. The crust is only 3 to 43 miles (5–69 km) thick. This layer of rock slides on top of the mantle. The bumps on the egg shell are like the mountains on Earth.

Moving Plates

We live on the outer layer of Earth, called the crust. The crust is broken into many pieces of rock, called plates. Earth's plates float on top of the mantle. They slide around very slowly on top of the molten rock. You can learn why the plates move slowly on the mantle by doing this experiment.

You will need

- a glass baking dish or a large bowl that is not too deep
- a spoon
- 3 cups (375 g) of cornstarch
- 2 ½ cups (592 ml) of water

1

Mix the cornstarch and the water in the bowl. When you mix two or more things together like this, it is called a mixture. It should be a little hard to mix but should not be dry.

2

Slowly stick your fingers in the bowl. What happens? Your fingers should sink in without any problem.

3

Pull your fingers out and let the mixture settle until the **surface** is flat again. Now take your hand and slap the surface of the mixture quickly. What happens? This time your hand should not go in the mixture because you moved quickly.

4

This mixture acts like Earth's mantle. If you try to move it quickly, it is hard. If you move it slowly, the mixture flows smoothly. The plates riding on Earth's mantle must move slowly for the same reason. If they tried to move quickly, the mantle would be too hard.

Day and Night

Everything in our solar system is continuously moving. Earth's movements explain why the Sun appears to move across the sky. They also explain why the Moon seems to change shape and why we have days and nights. Follow these steps to see why we have day and night.

You will need

- clay
- a pencil
- a flashlight
- a toothpick
- a friend

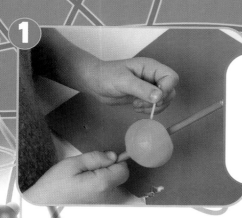

1 Shape the clay into a round ball to stand for Earth. Push the pencil through the middle of the ball so that it sticks out on both ends. The pencil stands for Earth's **axis**. Stick one end of the toothpick into the ball of clay to mark where you live.

2 Have a friend stand in the middle of the room holding a flashlight. Turn the flashlight on and shine it directly ahead. The flashlight stands for light from the Sun. Hold the ends of the pencil so that the clay Earth is in the light from the flashlight.

3 One side of the clay Earth is lit by the flashlight sun, making it daytime. The other side is dark, or nighttime. Is it daytime or nighttime where the toothpick is?

4 Slowly spin the pencil in your hands to move the toothpick through a day and a night. Watch the shadows made by the toothpick as it moves in and out of the flashlight's light. We see shadows like those on sunny days on Earth.

Making Waves

Oceans cover nearly three-quarters of Earth's surface. They are an important part of what makes our planet different from others. Earth's oceans are always on the move. Water flows beneath the surface. On the surface wind makes waves. You can see how waves work with this experiment.

You will need

- a bathtub or a sink full of water
- a plastic bottle cap or a cork
- a spoon

1

Fill a bathtub or sink with water. Then turn off the water and wait for it to settle. Softly place the bottle cap on top of the water in the middle of the bathtub or sink.

Near one end of the tub or sink, use a spoon to slap the surface of the water. Watch the bottle cap. Which way does it move? Does it move up and down? Does it move from side to side? Do not make too many waves or you will not see them well.

2

3

Remove the bottle cap from the tub or sink and wait for the water to settle. When there are no more waves, place the bottle cap in the water next to the side of the tub or sink.

4

Slap the surface of the water again to make waves. What happens to the bottle cap this time? As the waves near the edge of the tub or sink, they get broken up, just like waves hitting a dock or steep shoreline.

The **level** of the ocean water rises and falls on the beach each day. We call these changes in water level tides. Tides are caused by the Moon, which pulls on Earth. When the Moon is closest to one side of Earth, it pulls the water toward it and causes a high tide. Follow these steps to study the tides.

You will need

- a 1-quart (1 l) zip-seal bag
- an orange
- a cup
- 4 cups (1 l) solid vegetable shortening.
- a spoon

Fill the zip-seal bag about three-quarters full of vegetable shortening. The shortening is going to stand for the water in the ocean.

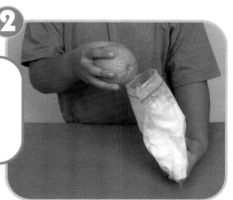

Place the orange in the bag. Move it around so it is covered in shortening. Seal the bag closed. The orange stands for Earth.

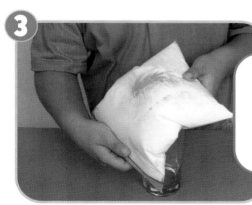

Set the orange on the rim of a cup and pretend you are the Moon. Which direction would the water in Earth's oceans be pulled?

Shape the bag so that the "water" is pulled toward you, the Moon. You should have a bump of vegetable shortening closest to you. "Earth" stays the same shape. If you change position, what happens to the "water"?

We need to take care of Earth. One way we can do this is by **recycling**. Part of our trash is made up of organic things, or things made from plants and animals. We can recycle this trash by composting. Composting turns organic trash into food for plants. You can start a compost pile in your own backyard.

You will need

- a space in the backyard, about the size of a bathtub
- four large rocks
- a shovel
- some soil
- water
- a ruler
- organic trash

1

Find a place in your backyard where an adult says it is okay to start a compost pile. Put one rock on each corner of the space where the compost pile will be. The rocks will help you keep the pile the right size.

Sort the organic trash from the rest of your trash. Make a layer of trash on the ground between the rocks. The layer should be no higher than 4 inches (10 cm).

2

3

Cover the layer with a shovelful of soil and spray with some water to make it wet. The soil and the water help bacteria and worms to break down the trash.

Every day add your organic trash to the pile and make a layer of soil and water. Use a shovel to turn the pile every two weeks. After three to six months, you should have fertilizer that can be used on plants in your yard. Fertilizer is food for plants.

4

Earth's atmosphere is made up of layers of air and gas around the planet. The air is important to people and animals because we breathe it to live. Sometimes, though, the air becomes polluted or dirty. **Chemicals**, dust, and smoke all pollute the air. You can do this easy experiment to see air pollution.

You will need

- four 3-by-5-inch (8 x 13 cm) paper cards
- a jar of petroleum jelly
- a butter knife or plastic knife
- four zip-seal sandwich bags
- a vacuum cleaner
- a dust rag

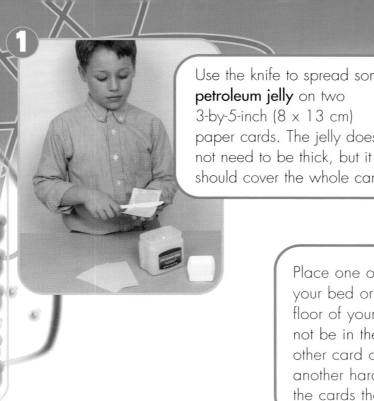

1

Use the knife to spread some **petroleum jelly** on two 3-by-5-inch (8 x 13 cm) paper cards. The jelly does not need to be thick, but it should cover the whole card.

2

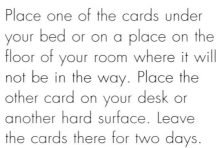

Place one of the cards under your bed or on a place on the floor of your room where it will not be in the way. Place the other card on your desk or another hard surface. Leave the cards there for two days.

3

Check the cards. There will likely be dust from the air trapped in the jelly. Does one have more dust than the other? Place each card in a zip-seal bag and save them.

4

Vacuum and dust your room and try the experiment again with the other two cards. What happens this time? Is there more dust on the two new cards than there is on the ones you used before cleaning? What does this tell you about the air after cleaning your room?

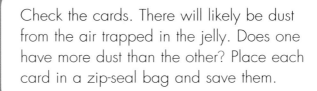

Earth Science, All Science

Wow! There really is so much to learn about Earth. We have just gotten started. All kinds of scientists study different parts of our world. Some study the oceans. Some study the rocks. Some study the living things on Earth. Other scientists study the weather or the atmosphere.

No matter what scientists study, they are all trying to find answers about Earth. What do you want to find out next?

Glossary

axis (AK-sus) A line around which an object turns or seems to turn.

chemicals (KEH-mih-kulz) Matter that can be mixed with other matter to cause changes.

core (KOR) The hot center of Earth.

crust (KRUST) The outer, or top, layer of a planet.

energy (EH-nur-jee) The power to work or to act.

experiments (ek-SPER-uh-ments) Sets of actions or steps taken to learn more about something.

level (LEH-vul) How high something reaches.

mantle (MAN-tul) The middle layer of Earth.

petroleum jelly (peh-TROH-lee-um JEH-lee) A thick spread made from oil that is used to keep skin safe.

planet (PLA-net) A large object, such as Earth, that moves around the Sun.

recycling (ree-SY-kling) Using things again instead of throwing them out.

scientists (SY-un-tists) People who study the world by using tests and experiments.

solar system (SOH-ler SIS-tem) A group of planets that circles a star.

surface (SER-fes) The outside of anything.

vacuum (VA-kyoom) To use a machine that cleans floors and rugs by sucking in the dirt.

Index

Web Sites

Due to the changing nature of Internet links, PowerKids Press has developed an online list of Web sites related to the subject of this book. This site is updated regularly. Please use this link to access the list:
www.powerkidslinks.com/diysci/earth/